Emergency! Be Prepared

Lisa Greathouse

Consultant

Gina Montefusco, RN
Children's Hospital Los Angeles
Los Angeles, California

Publishing Credits

Dona Herweck Rice, *Editor-in-Chief*
Lee Aucoin, *Creative Director*
Don Tran, *Print Production Manager*
Timothy J. Bradley, *Illustration Manager*
Chris McIntyre, M.A.Ed., *Editorial Director*
James Anderson, M.S.Ed., *Editor*
Stephanie Reid, *Photo Editor*
Rachelle Cracchiolo, M.S.Ed., *Publisher*

Image Credits

Cover Stephanie Reid; p.1 Stephanie Reid; p.4 Roger Mcclean/Dreamstime.com; p.5(left) Yuri Arcurs/Shutterstock; p.5(right) MedicalRF.com/Photolibrary.com; p.6 Pöllö/Wikipedia; p.7 Anette Linnea Rasmussen/Shutterstock; p.8 Jan Kranendonk/iStockphoto; p.9(top) Roger Jegg/Shutterstock; p.9(bottom) John Sartin/Shutterstock; p.10 La Fabrika Pixel S.l./Dreamstime.com; p.11 Getty Images/Collection Mix: Subjects RM; p.12 iofoto/Shutterstock; p.13(top) Paul Gunning/Photo Researchers, Inc.; p.13(bottom) BSIP/Photo Researchers, Inc.; p.14 Sebastian Kaulitzki/Shutterstock; p.15(left) ZUMA Press/Newscom; p.16 Chuck Swartzell/Visuals Unlimited/Corbis; p.17(top) SentientPhotos/Bigstock; p.17(bottom left) Grace Alba; p.17(bottom right) Faye Norman/Photo Researchers, Inc.; p.18(top) David Scharf/Photo Researchers, Inc.; p.18(bottom) Gayvoronskaya_yana/Shutterstock; p.19 Avid Creative, Inc./iStockphoto; p.20 gmwnz/Shutterstock; p.21(top) Candace Schwadron/Shutterstock; p.21(bottom left) Tihis/Shutterstock; p.21(bottom right) Edward Shaw/iStockphoto; p.22(top left) luminouslens/Shutterstock; p.22(top right) TCM; p.22(bottom) Max Lowry/Shutterstock; p.23 Richard T. Nowitz/CORBIS; p.24 m.bonotto/Shutterstock; p.25 Marc van Vuren/Shutterstock; p.26 Morgan Lane Photography/Shutterstock; p.27(top) Sashkin/Shutterstock; p.27(bottom) Julia Nichols/iStockphoto; pp.28–29(all) Nicolle Rager Fuller; p.32(top) k03/ZUMA Press/Newscom; p.32(bottom) prism68/Shutterstock; Back cover iofoto/Shutterstock

---

Teacher Created Materials
5301 Oceanus Drive
Huntington Beach, CA 92649-1030
http://www.tcmpub.com

ISBN 978-1-4333-3092-6

Table of Contents

Do Not Panic!

Imagine that you and a friend are riding your bikes. You hear a loud noise and turn around to see your friend's bike on the ground. Then you see your friend lying nearby. He is not moving, but you hear him groaning. You remember seeing a deep pothole in the road a few seconds earlier, but you had swerved to avoid it. Your friend must not have seen it in time and was thrown from his bike.

You race over and see he is bleeding. His leg is bent in a weird way. He starts to cry. It feels like your heart is beating out of your chest. You tell your friend that everything will be okay, but you are not so sure. What do you do?

Did You Know?

More than 275,000 kids under the age of 14 are injured in bike accidents every year in the United States. Many of them involve head injuries. That is why you should always wear a helmet when bike riding. In many countries, it is the law!

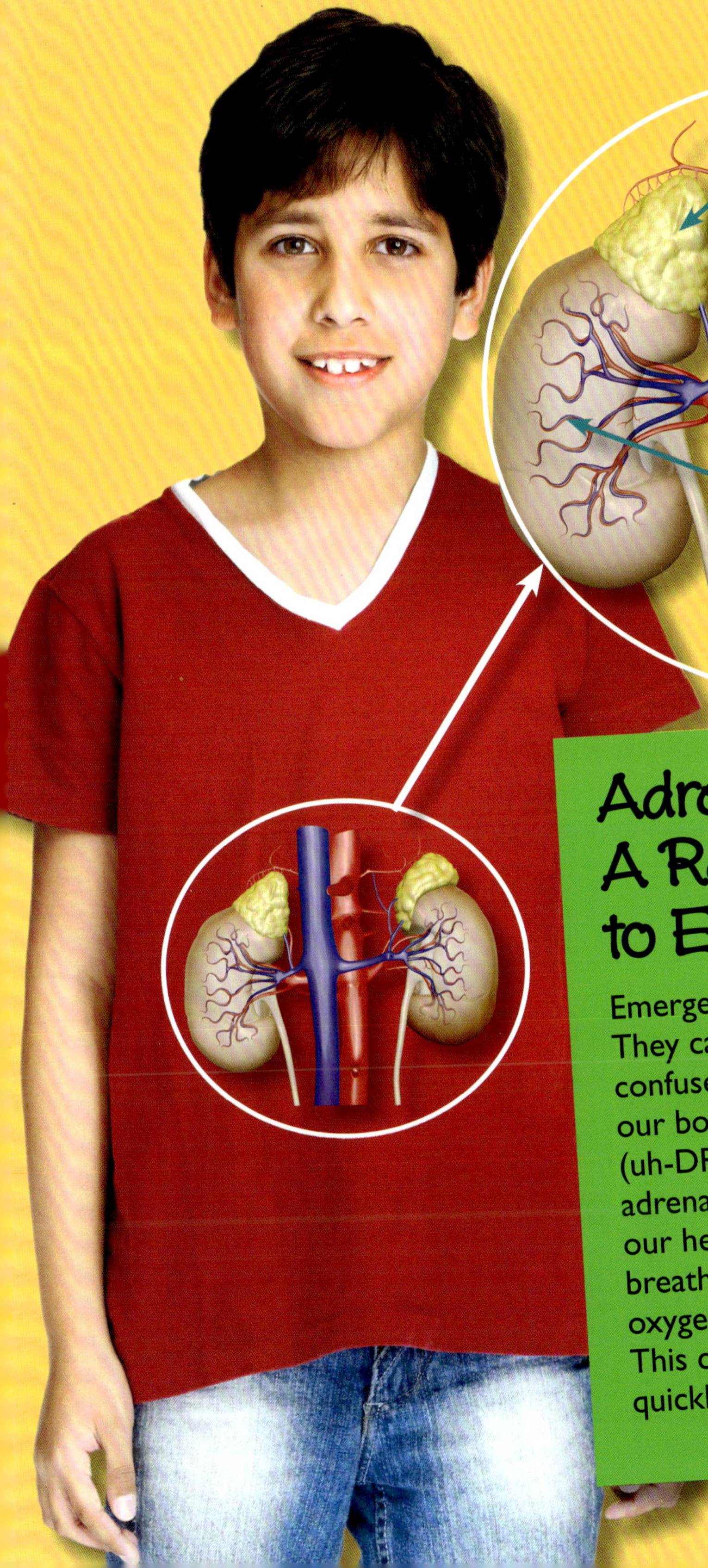

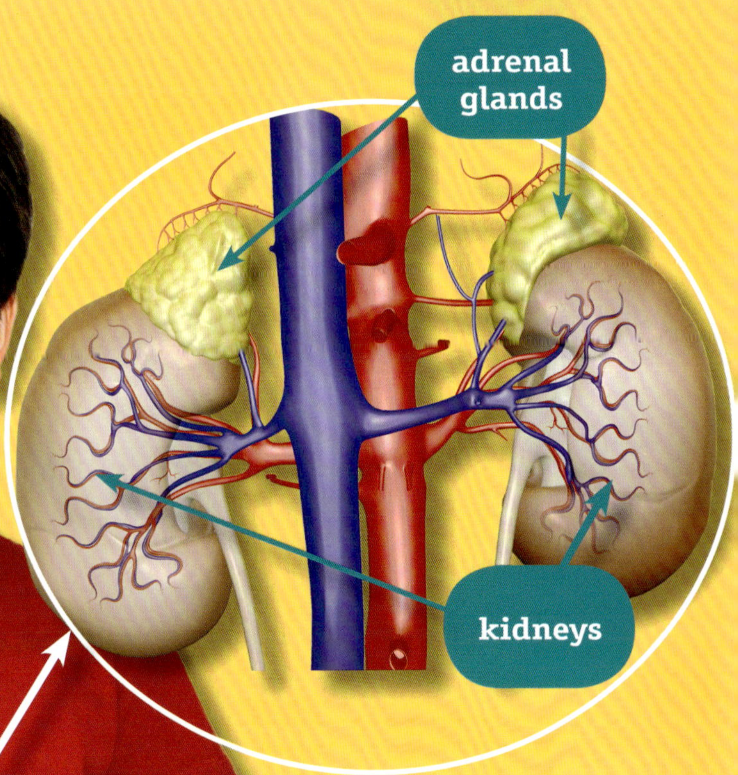

Adrenaline: A Response to Emergency

Emergencies can be stressful. They can make us feel afraid or confused. When this happens our bodies release **adrenaline** (uh-DREN-ul-in) from our adrenal glands. Adrenaline raises our heart rates. It makes us breathe more. This causes more oxygen to move to our muscles. This can help us react to danger quickly and with more energy.

Call for Help

When you face an **emergency** alone, you need help. You need to tell an adult. If you are near a phone, call emergency services. In the United States, that number is 9-1-1.

A **dispatcher** will pick up your call. This police officer will call other officers and emergency teams. You may need a fire truck. You may need an ambulance. The dispatcher will send them to you. He or she will ask you questions. Your answers are important. The officer wants to send you the right kind of help. Take a deep breath. Then, answer as clearly as you can. That is not easy when you are scared and upset! Stay calm. It is the best way to get help fast.

emergency dispatch office

Did You Know?

9-1-1 is not the emergency number in all countries. In Australia, it is 0-0-0. In Sudan, the number is 9-9-9.

Calling for Help

When you leave your home, it is a good idea to take along a cell phone if you can. That way, you can call for help if you need it. Remember, only call 9-1-1 if you think someone's life may be in danger.

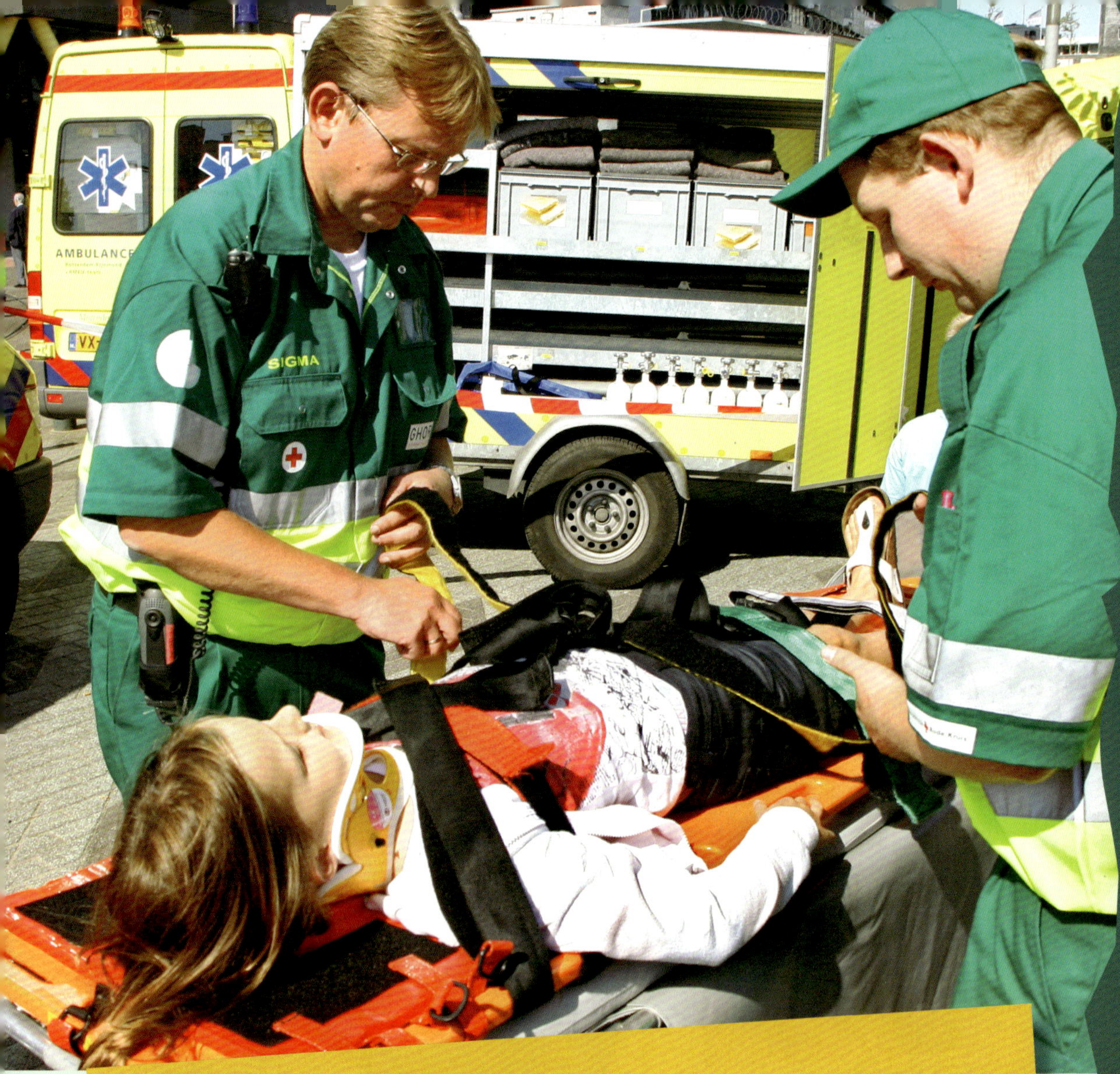

Move to Safety

It is important not to move an injured person if you can help it. Serious injuries can be made worse if the injured person moves. This is especially true for neck or spine injuries that can leave a person **paralyzed**, or unable to move. However, if a person can walk, help him out of harm's way. If he is injured in the middle of the street, you do not want him (or you!) to get hit by a car.

What if you do not have a cell phone? You still need help from an adult. If the injury is serious, it may not be safe to leave your friend and go for help. Try yelling for help. Someone may hear you and come to your aid. If you are near a road, try to flag down a car. Wave your arms and shout.

If someone comes out of a house or stops in a car, ask him or her to call an ambulance.

This person will most likely be a stranger. Do not accept a ride or go into a stranger's house. It is okay if this person waits outside with you until help comes. If no one answers your cries for help, do not just stay put. In this case, make sure your friend is safe. Then, go to find help.

interior of an ambulance

First Aid

Emergencies do not happen often. When people get hurt, they rarely need an ambulance. For example, if you fall off your bike, you may just scrape a knee or bruise an elbow. If so, go home so an adult can clean your **wound** and put a bandage on it.

You can do basic first aid. First, rinse a wound with clean water. Then, put a clean paper towel or a washcloth over the wound. Press down with your hand over the paper towel or cloth and wound. That will help stop the bleeding. You can also use a T-shirt or any clean piece of cloth to stop the bleeding. Have an adult or a doctor look at the wound as soon as possible.

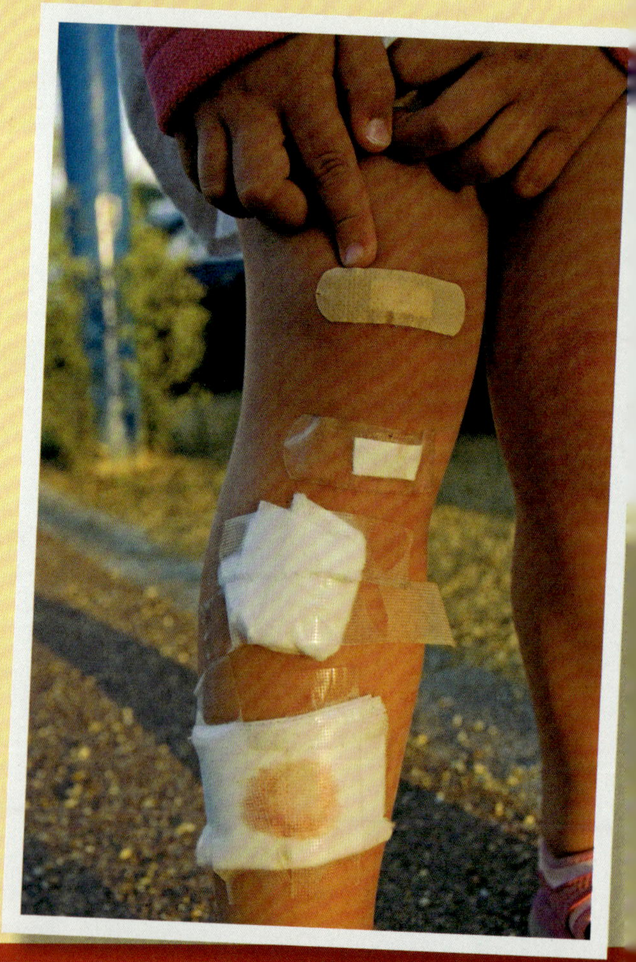

If you are treating another person's wound, do not touch their blood. Blood can carry diseases. So, be sure to wear rubber gloves while you are helping them.

Burn!

Have you ever accidentally touched a hot oven or an iron? Ouch! Burns are pretty common injuries. If you have just a minor burn, follow these tips:

1. Hold the area under cool running water for 10 minutes.
2. Cover the burn with a sterile (STER-il), or clean, bandage.
3. Raise the covered burn area above your heart to reduce the swelling.

If it is a more serious burn and your skin has blistered, do not use any bandage material that is fluffy or it will stick to the wound. If no sterile bandage can be found, wrap the wound in ordinary plastic wrap. This will keep the wound clean and bound until you get to the hospital.

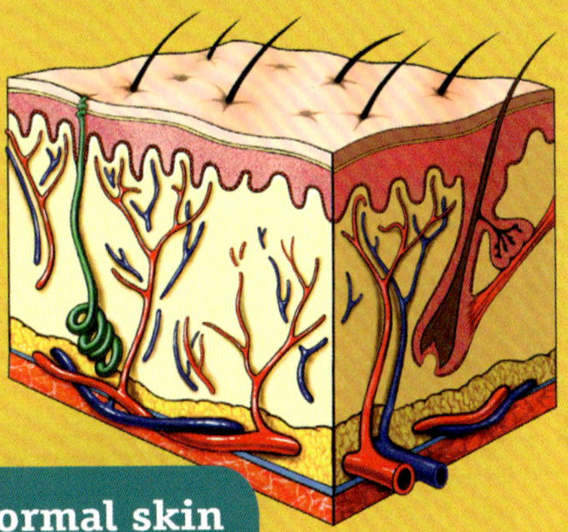

normal skin

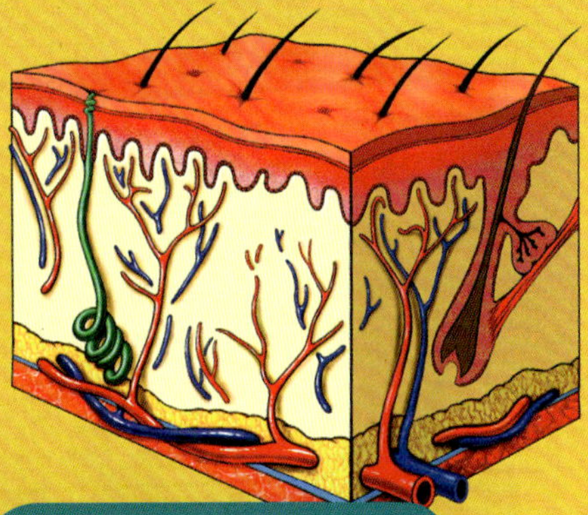

first-degree burn

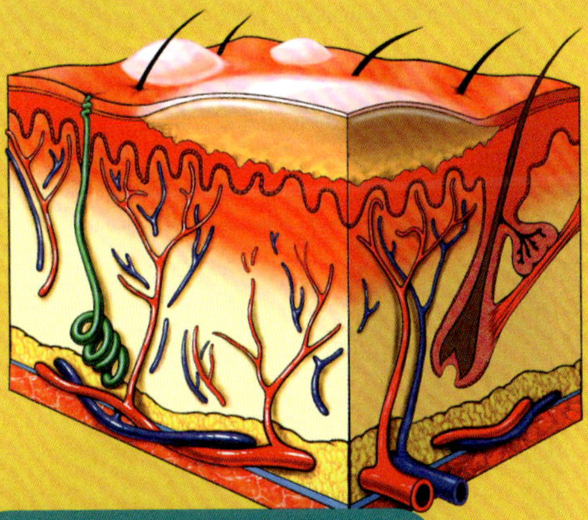

second-degree burn

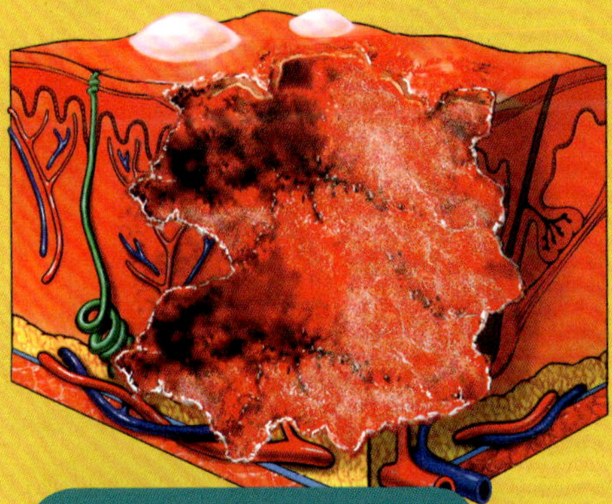

third-degree burn

Some injuries may need medical attention. But that does not make them an emergency. Maybe you bumped your head and would like to have it looked at by a doctor. Or maybe you broke your finger or sprained a wrist. Although these injuries are painful, they are not life threatening. When such injuries happen, tell your parents. They may take you to a hospital, urgent care, or your doctor.

Not all emergencies can be **prevented**. But many can be. You need to use your head and follow basic safety rules.

Nature's Bandage

When you get a scrape or a cut your wound starts to bleed. That is when your body snaps into action. When your blood is exposed to the air, your body sends **white blood cells** to clean the wound and fight infection. Your body also makes a protein called **fibrin**. Fibrin forms a mesh over your wound and clots, or blocks, the blood cells that are trying to escape. When it dries, it forms a scab.

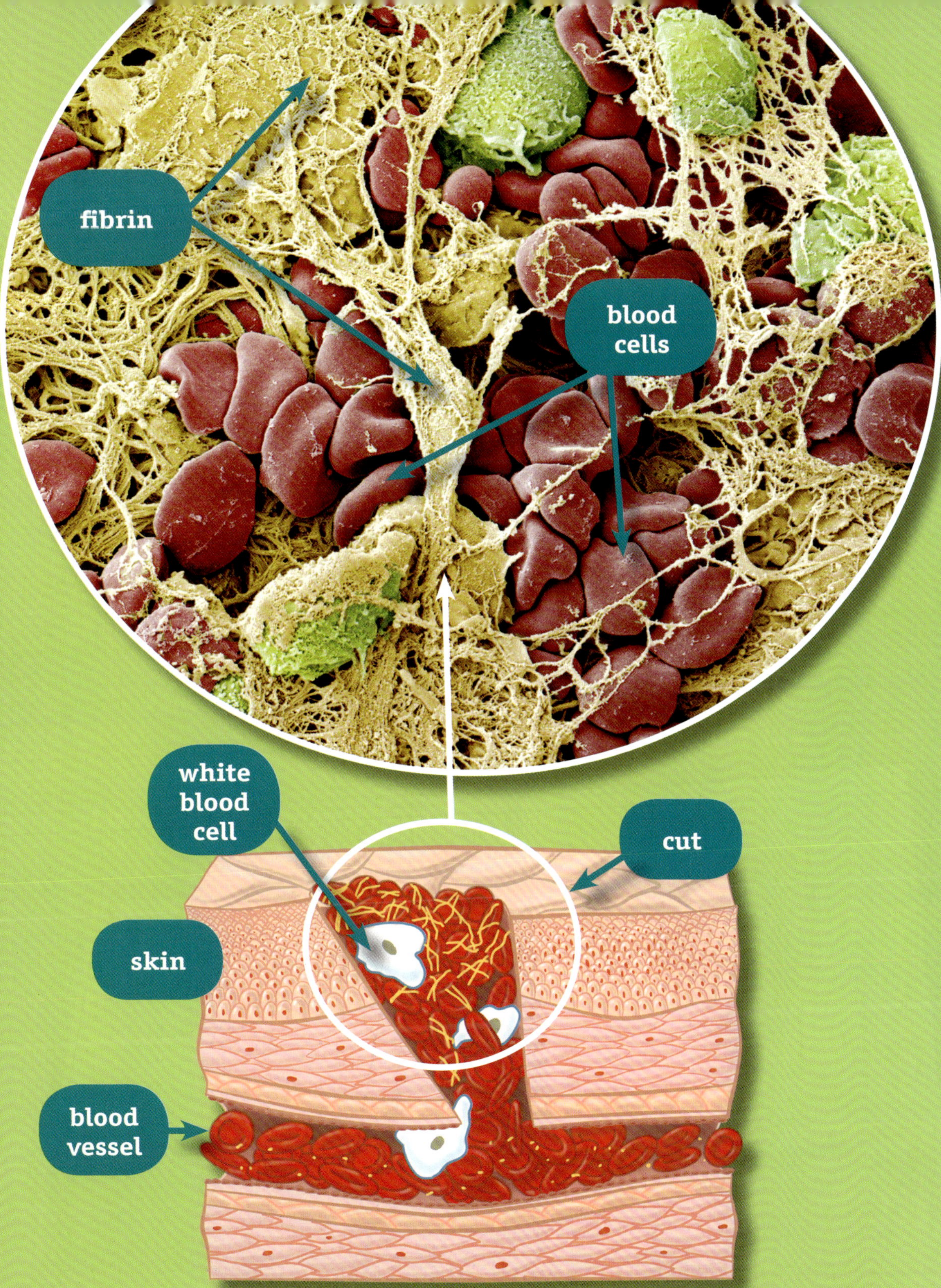
fibrin
blood cells
white blood cell
cut
skin
blood vessel

CPR Saves Lives

You may have seen it on TV or in the movies. Someone collapses or is pulled from the water. They are not breathing. "Who knows CPR?" someone yells.

CPR stands for **cardiopulmonary resuscitation** (kar-dee-o-PUHL-muh-ner-ee ri-SUHS-i-tey-shun). There are two parts to CPR. First, a person breathes into the victim's mouth. Next, the person presses on the victim's chest. Then the steps are repeated.

CPR may save a person who is not breathing or whose heart has stopped beating. If you see this kind of emergency, seek help from an adult trained in CPR. Better yet, call for an ambulance. But you can learn CPR, too. You never know when a medical emergency will happen. It is great to be able to help.

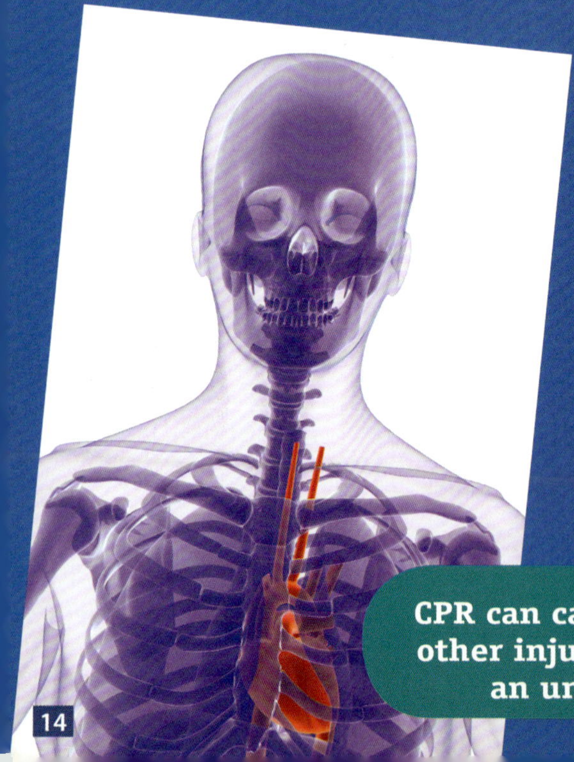

CPR can cause broken ribs and other injuries if performed by an untrained person.

CPR cards tell the world that you know how to save lives!

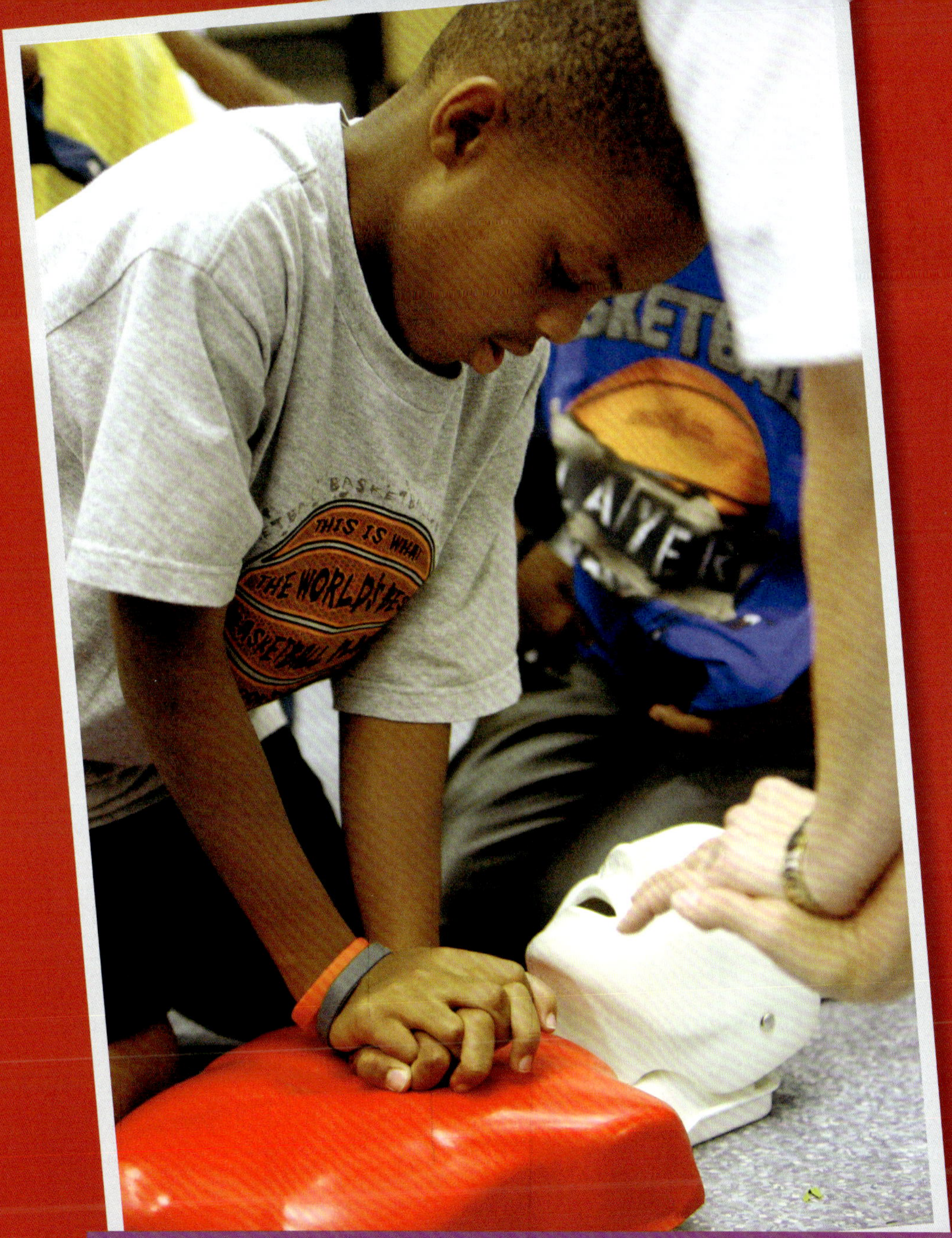

Be a Lifesaver!

Talk to your parents about taking a CPR class. Many groups such as the American Red Cross offer classes. Check if your local hospital, fire department, YMCA, church, or school offers any classes. Your parents can get trained, too!

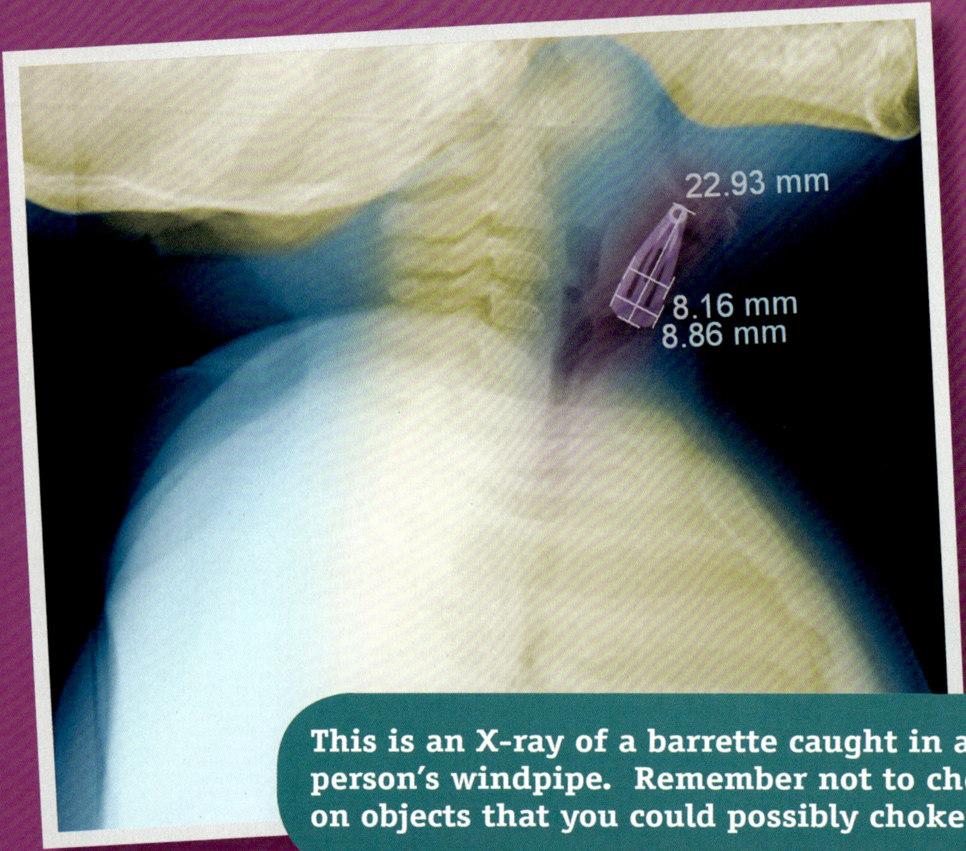

This is an X-ray of a barrette caught in a person's windpipe. Remember not to chew on objects that you could possibly choke on.

Choking Rescue

When you were little, your parents cut up your food into small pieces. That was because your throat was small. It was about the size of your little finger. Your parents did not want food to get caught in your throat. Then you might **choke**.

Choking is a danger to people of all ages. If you have ever choked, you know how scary it is. You cannot cough, speak, or breathe. You need help fast. If you choke, put both of your hands around your neck. This lets others know that you need help.

If you see someone choking, call an ambulance. Then, help the choking person. Give him or her the Heimlich maneuver. Here is how:

- Stand behind the person.
- Make a fist with your thumb sticking up.
- Put your thumb against the person's stomach, just under his or her rib cage.
- Place your other hand over your fist.
- Pull your fist up and in with force.

Use your hands to show others you are choking.

the Heimlich maneuver in action

Food Poisoning!

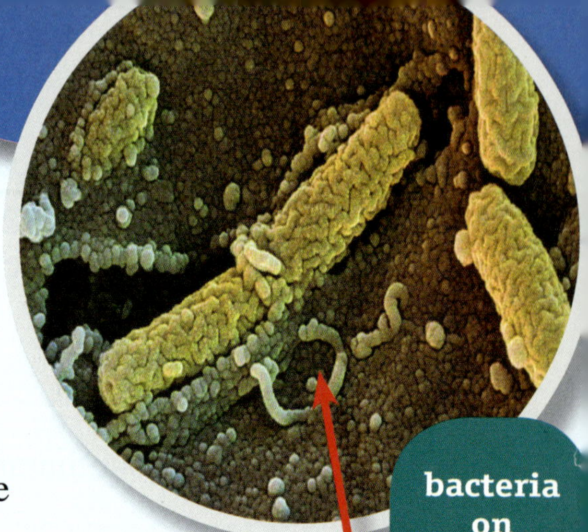

bacteria on uncooked meat

Has food ever made you sick? If it has, you may have had **food poisoning**. This happens when germs get in your food. These germs make the food bad for you.

If you have food poisoning, you will feel sick to your stomach. You may vomit or even have diarrhea (dahy-uh-REE-uh). But do not panic. There are steps you can take to make yourself well again. First, see a doctor as soon as possible. A doctor will be able to tell you if your illness is serious. And getting a checkup when you are ill is always a good idea.

Food poisoning makes your body lose a lot of liquid, so be sure to drink plenty of water. Also, give your stomach a break and only eat bland foods. This will reduce the chance of vomiting.

Poison at Home

Did you know there are poisons in your home? We use some of them to clean. We use others to keep our cars working. Even medicine can be poison if it is not taken the way a doctor tells you to. Around 90 percent of poisonings in the U.S. happen in the home. Poison can get into our bodies if we eat, touch, or smell it. Keep things that are poisons in a safe place. If you do swallow poison, call 9-1-1 or your local Poison Control Center right away.

Water Safety Basics

When the weather warms up, what is more fun than a day at the beach or a jump in the pool? But **drowning** is a leading cause of death among children. And it can happen in just minutes. Learning these water-safety basics can help prevent you from getting hurt:

- Never swim alone. There should always be a grown-up around. And you should always swim with a buddy.
- At the beach, swim where a lifeguard can see you.
- Look before you dive. Diving is dangerous if the water is not deep enough. Ask an adult or look at the markers on the sides of a pool to see if it is safe to dive.
- Obey pool rules. And at the beach, listen to the lifeguard's warnings.

This Myth Is All Wet!

Have you ever heard the warning that you need to wait an hour to swim after you have eaten? The thinking was that you could get cramps and drown. But experts say that this advice is a myth. Feel free to have lunch or a snack before jumping in!

Surviving Disaster

Disasters can happen at any time. And we cannot always tell when they will occur. But we can prepare for an emergency. You can get ready for earthquakes, fires, tornadoes, and hurricanes. You can prepare the things that you would need for these events. Read the rest of this book. It will tell you what to do if disaster strikes.

Fire!

We all need fire to live. It gives us warmth. It **purifies**, or cleans, our water. It cooks our food. But fire can be hot, loud, and scary. It can destroy homes in minutes. And it can kill. In fact, fire is one of the top causes of serious injuries for children. That is why it is important for you to learn what to do in case of a fire.

Of course, the best thing to do is avoid fire. Use matches, lighters, and candles only with adult help. Test the smoke alarms in your house often. Do not leave a fire unattended when you are cooking. Cooking is the main cause of house fires. Keep a fire extinguisher near the kitchen, just in case.

Fire escape ladders can help you escape a fire when you are not on the ground floor of a building.

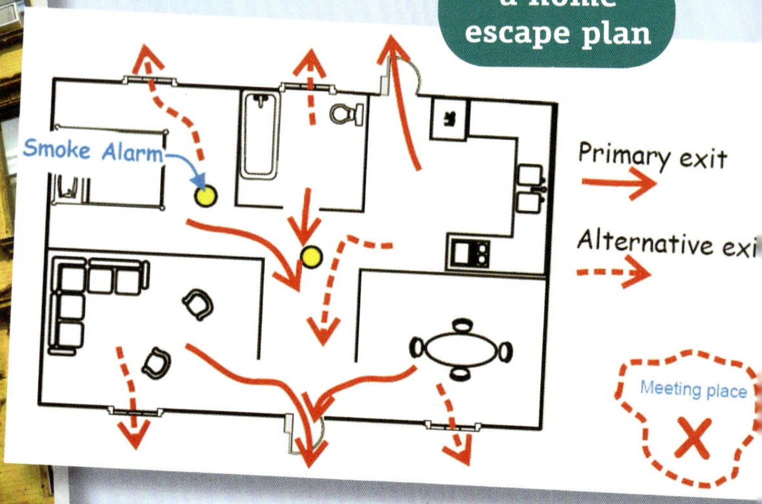

a home escape plan

Seeing Spots!

Why is it that Dalmatians are the **mascots** of the firehouse? It is partly because Dalmatians and horses get along well. Long ago, firefighters used horse-drawn fire carts. Dalmatians were trained to run in front of the horses to clear a path and get the firefighters to the fires quickly.

What should you do if you hear the smoke alarm in your home or smell smoke? Fires move fast. So you must act fast! You need to practice before a fire breaks out.

In a fire, smoke can make your home very dark. That is why your family needs to have an escape plan. Smoke rises. So stay low to the floor to escape. You may need to crawl to an exit. If you have to open any doors, test the doorknob first. If it is hot, do not open it. This heat means there is fire on the other side of the door. After you get out of your home, call the fire department.

You might want to take your favorite belongings. But nothing you own is as important as your life. Get out as fast as you can. Even if you forget something, do not go back inside.

Natural Disasters

There are all sorts of **natural disasters**. There are earthquakes and wildfires. There are hurricanes and tornadoes. There are also floods. We get warned before some disasters, like hurricanes. Others, like earthquakes, strike with no warning. Natural disasters can ruin homes and cause deaths.

So what do you do during a natural disaster? One thing you should do is stay calm. You should also listen to and follow the directions your parents give you.

A rescue dog helps an emergency worker find survivors of a large earthquake.

Survivors in Indonesia wade through a flood caused by a tsunami.

But what if you are by yourself when disaster strikes? During an earthquake, find a sturdy structure. This can be something such as a table. Then, crawl under and hold onto it. Protect your head and neck with your arms. Do this until the earthquake stops. Then, move outdoors and away from any buildings or power lines. During a flood, move to higher ground and wait for help. Stay out of the water. If there is a swift current, it may sweep you away. If you see a wildfire approaching, call 9-1-1 right away. Then **evacuate**. Move as far away from the fire as possible.

Pet Supply Kit

Most of us think of our pets as part of the family. That is why you should also put together an emergency supply kit for your four-legged friends. That means a three-day supply of pet food and water. Your pet should also wear an ID tag in case it runs away during an emergency situation.

Be Prepared

It is scary to think about emergencies. Sometimes you can avoid them by being careful. Other times, there is nothing you can do to stop them. Some emergencies just happen. And you must act fast. If you are prepared, you can make a difference. It may be as simple as making an emergency supply kit. Or it may mean testing your smoke alarms. Maybe it is taking a class on how to do CPR. If you know what to do in an emergency, you might even save a life!

An emergency supply kit should include:

- ☑ A flashlight, radio, and two sets of batteries
- ☑ A three-day supply of **nonperishable** food for each family member
- ☑ Three gallons of water for each family member
- ☑ A change of clothing for every family member
- ☑ A first-aid kit
- ☑ Blankets or sweaters

The Doctor Is In

Dr. Mehmet Oz doesn't *play* a doctor on TV. He really is a heart surgeon. But, most people know him as a TV talk show host. Dr. Oz's goal is simple. He wants to help people lead long and healthy lives.

Dr. Oz shows how eating healthy foods and being fit are the two keys to good health. But he teaches other healthy habits, too. Dr. Oz teaches everything from how to brush your teeth the right way to what to do in a medical emergency.

People from all over the world ask Dr. Oz questions about their health. No wonder his show wins awards and his books are bestsellers!

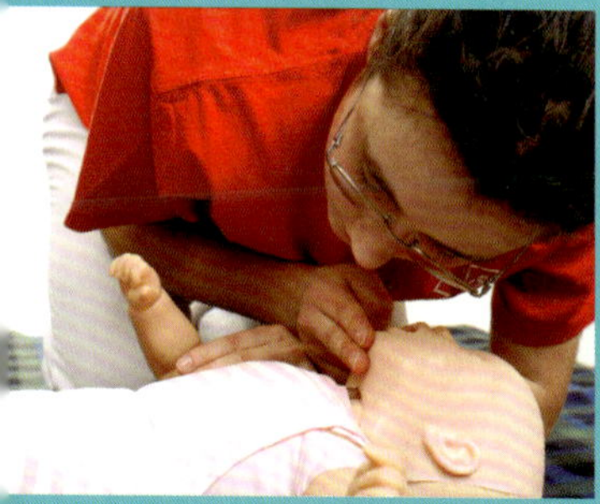

Personal Challenge

Ask your parents to sign you up for a first aid or CPR course. Then ask a friend to sign up with you. You never know when you might be able to help save a life!